Through the Heart of the Jungle

For Laura, who roared at the mother asleep in her bed – J.E

To the two little monkeys I know, Andrew and Ryan Pink – E.G

THROUGH THE HEART OF THE JUNGLE
by Jonathan Emmett and Elena Gomez

British Library Cataloguing in Publication Data
A catalogue record of this book is available from
the British Library.
ISBN 0 340 85439 1 (HB)
ISBN 0 340 85440 5 (PB)

First edition published 2003
10 9 8 7 6 5 4 3 2 1

Published by Hodder Children's Books
a division of Hodder Headline Limited
338 Euston Road London NW1 3BH

Printed in Hong Kong

You can find out more about Jonathan Emmett's books
by visiting his web site at www.scribblestreet.co.uk

Through the Heart of the Jungle

Written by Jonathan Emmett
Illustrated by Elena Gomez

Hodder
Children's
Books

A division of Hodder Headline Limited

This is the heart of the jungle.

This is the fly,

That buzzed through the heart of the jungle.

That buzzed through the heart of the jungle.

This is the toad with the big beady eye,

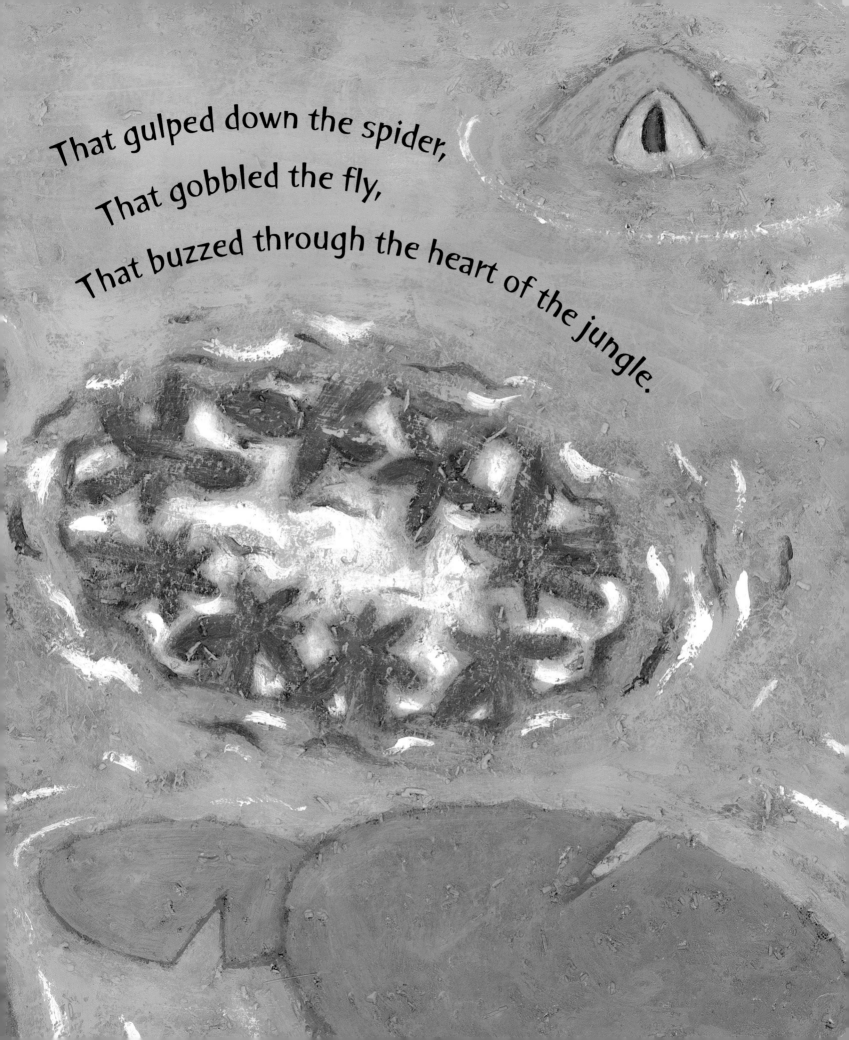

That gulped down the spider,
That gobbled the fly,
That buzzed through the heart of the jungle.

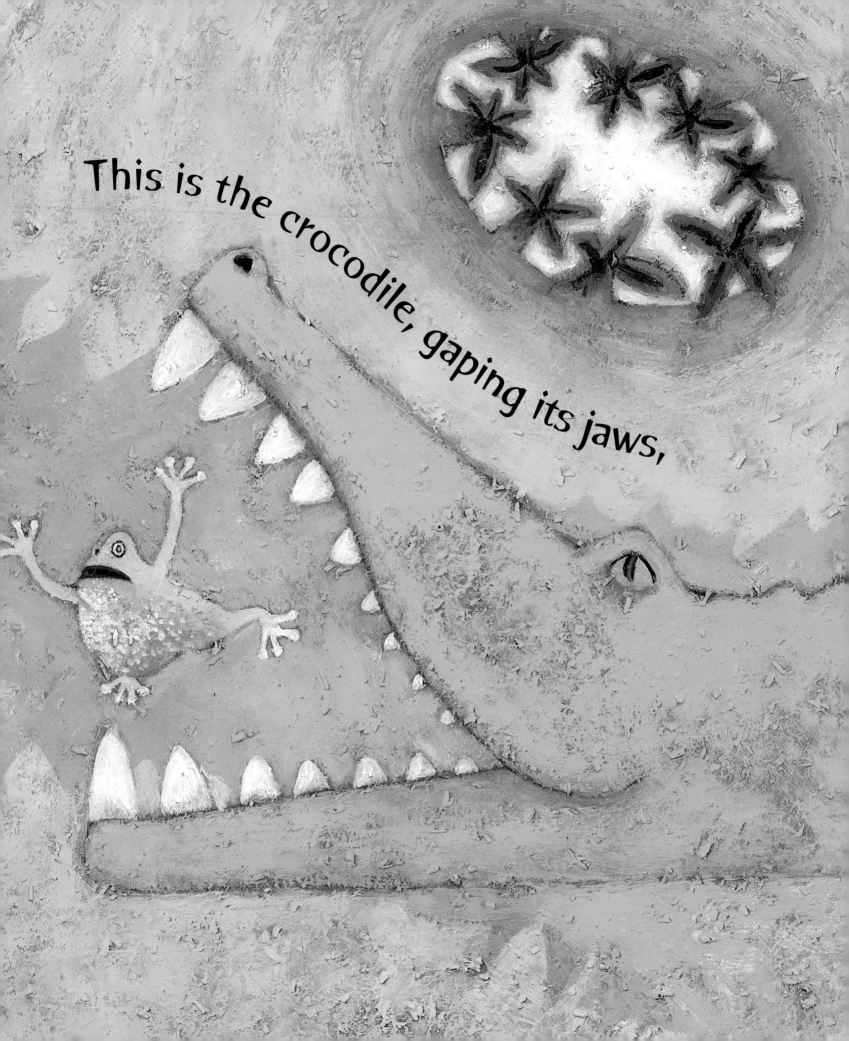

That snapped at the toad with the big beady eye,
That gulped down the spider,
That gobbled the fly,
That buzzed through the heart of the jungle.

This is the bear with the
long pointy claws,

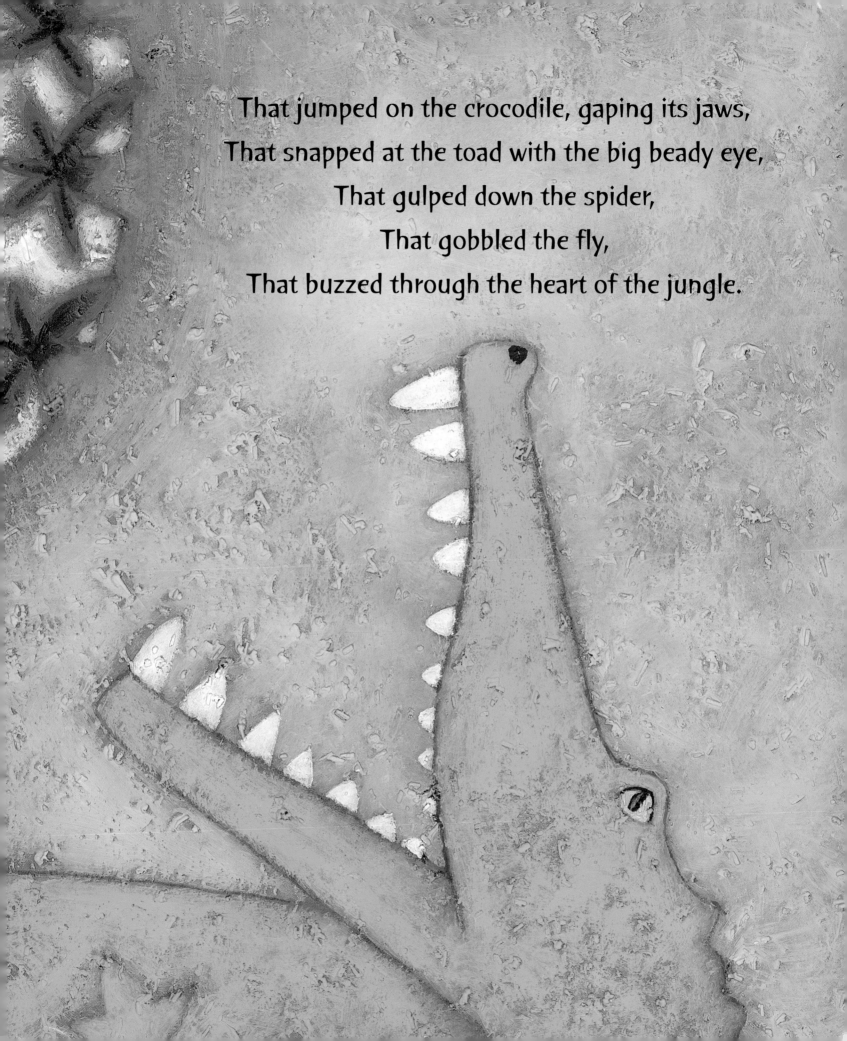

That jumped on the crocodile, gaping its jaws,

That snapped at the toad with the big beady eye,

That gulped down the spider,

That gobbled the fly,

That buzzed through the heart of the jungle.

This is the monkey that let out a shriek,

That startled the bear with the long pointy claws,

That jumped on the crocodile, gaping its jaws,

That snapped at the toad with the big beady eye,

That gulped down the spider,

That gobbled the fly,

That buzzed through the heart of the jungle.

This is the bird with the bright orange beak,

That flew at the monkey that let out a shriek,

That startled the bear with the long pointy claws,

That jumped on the crocodile, gaping its jaws,

That snapped at the toad with the big beady eye,

That gulped down the spider,

That gobbled the fly,

That buzzed through the heart of the jungle.

This is the snake that slithered and slunk,

That hissed at the bird with the bright orange beak,

That flew at the monkey that let out a shriek,

That startled the bear with the long pointy claws,

That jumped on the crocodile, gaping its jaws,

That snapped at the toad with the big beady eye,

That gulped down the spider,

That gobbled the fly,

That buzzed through the heart of the jungle.

This is the elephant, swinging its trunk,

That swatted the snake that slithered and slunk,

That hissed at the bird with the bright orange beak,

That flew at the monkey that let out a shriek,

That startled the bear with the long pointy claws,

That jumped on the crocodile, gaping its jaws,

That snapped at the toad with the big beady eye,

That gulped down the spider,

That gobbled the fly,

That buzzed through the heart of the jungle.

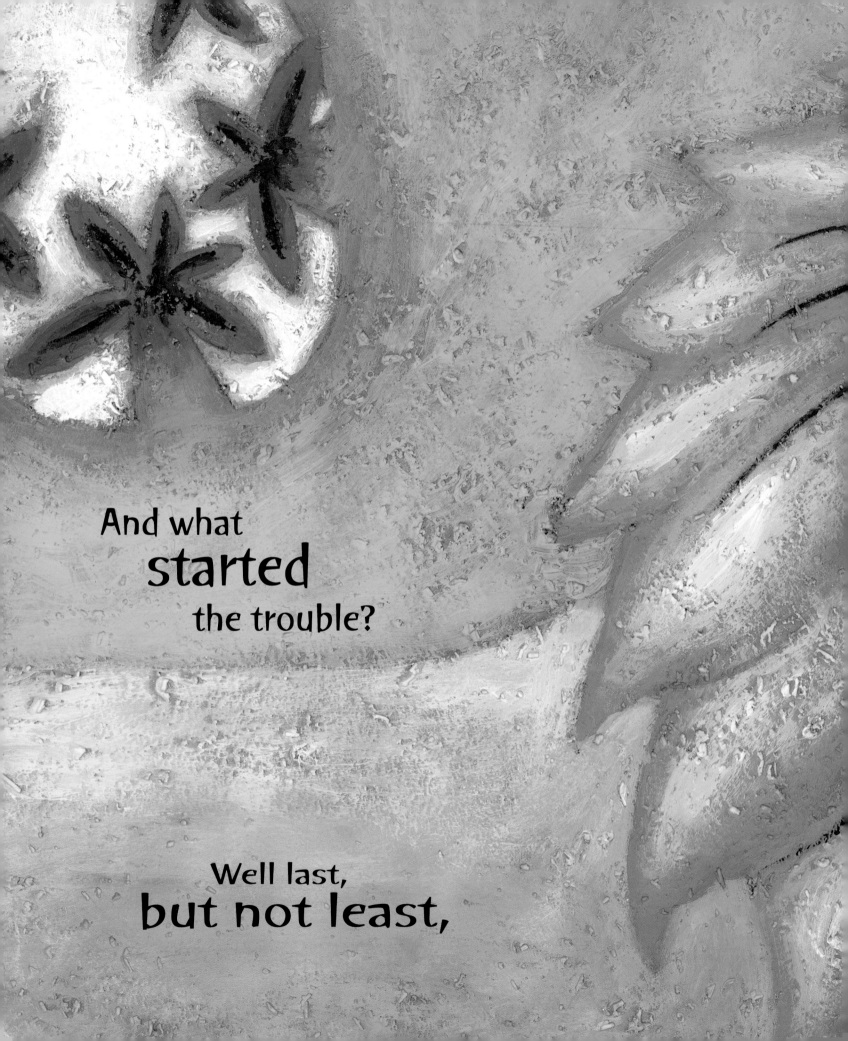

And what **started** the trouble?

Well last, **but not least,**

This is the lion, the king of the beasts,

That roared at
the elephant,
swinging its trunk,

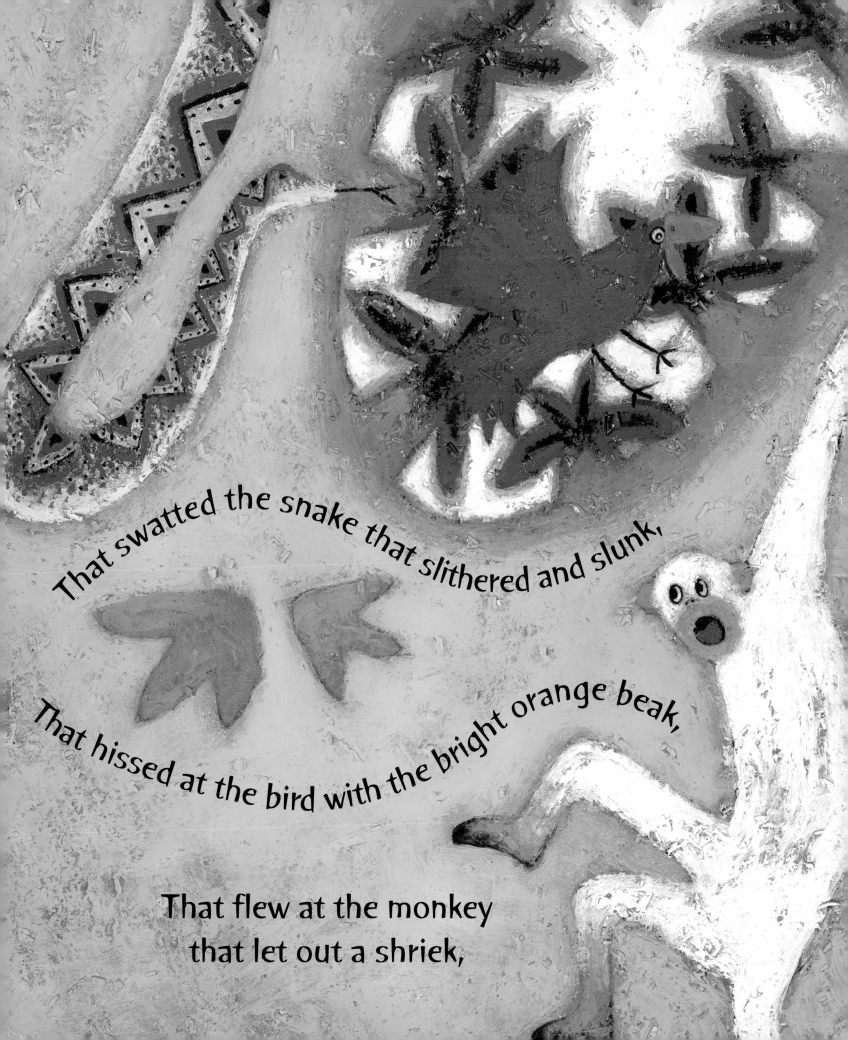

That swatted the snake that slithered and slunk,

That hissed at the bird with the bright orange beak,

That flew at the monkey
that let out a shriek,

That startled
the bear
with the
long
pointy
claws,

That jumped on the crocodile, gaping its jaws,

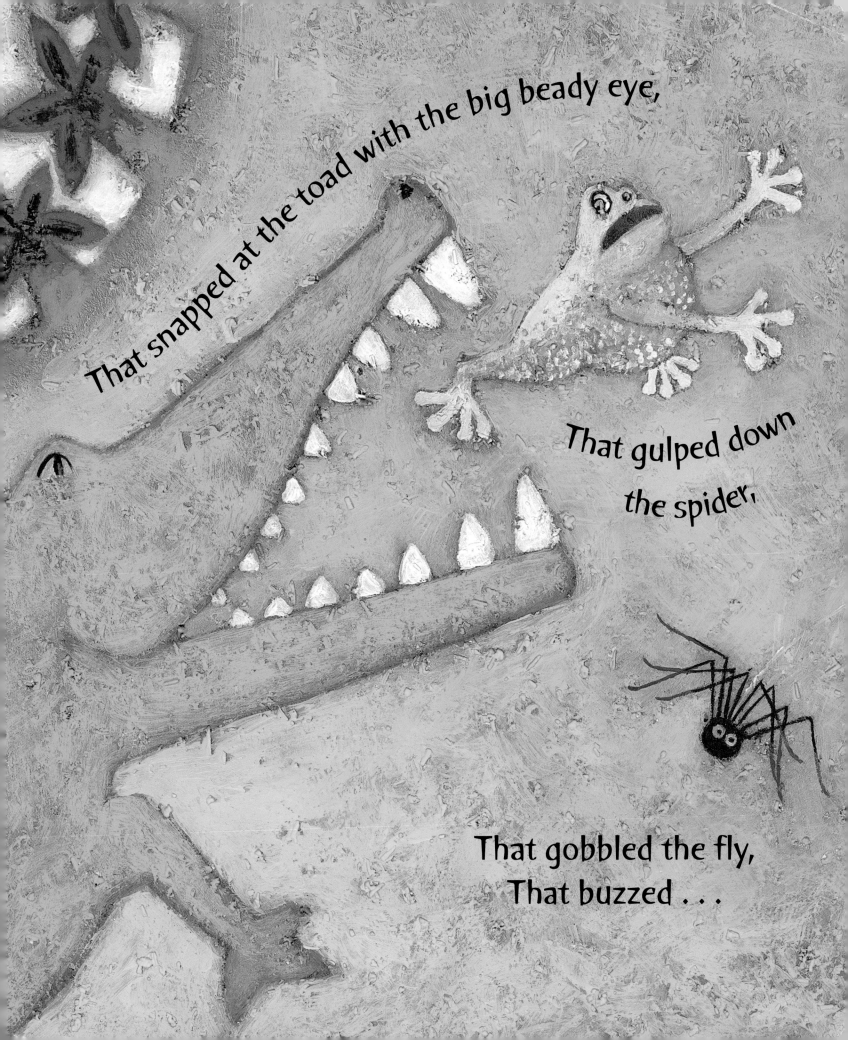

... through the heart of the jungle!